Text Copyright © 1987 by Selina Hastings
Illustration Copyright © 1987 by Reg Cartwright
All rights reserved, including the right to reproduce
this book or portions thereof in any form.
First published 1987 in Great Britain by
Walker Books Ltd., London.
Published in the United States by
Henry Holt and Company, Inc., 521 Fifth Avenue,
New York, New York 10175.

Library of Congress Cataloging in Publication Data
Hastings, Selina.
Peter and the wolf.
Summary: Retells the orchestral fairy tale of the
boy who, ignoring his grandfather's warnings, proceeds
to capture a wolf.
[1. Fairy tales]   I. Cartwright, Reg, ill.
II. Prokofiev, Sergei, 1891–1953.   Petīa i volk.
III. Title.
PZ8.H265Pe 1987   [E]   86-27004
ISBN 0-8050-0408-4

First American Edition

Printed in Hong Kong by South China Printing Company
1 3 5 7 9 10 8 6 4 2

Peter and the Wolf

Retold by Selina Hastings
Illustrated by Reg Cartwright

Based on the Orchestral Tale
by Sergei Prokofiev

Henry Holt and Company · New York

Peter lived with his grandfather in a little house in the middle of one of the great Russian forests. The forest was a dark and dangerous place, and on still nights the howling of wolves rose clearly into the air. But Peter's home was in a pleasant clearing. It was surrounded by a garden and a high stone wall. Outside the wall were a meadow and a pond and every morning Peter would come whistling down the path and through the gate into the meadow, his pockets full of bread for the duck who lived on the pond.

One morning Peter came down to the pond as usual. In the overhanging branches of a tree a hungry bird waited for crumbs to fall from Peter's hands. At his feet sat an old gray cat, eyes fixed intently on the bird. But Peter's attention was on the duck, paddling around and around the center of the pond, greedily gobbling up the morsels of bread. He didn't notice the cat, now lying at the foot of the tree. The bird didn't notice either as she hopped up and down on her branch, beadily watching for the moment when she could snatch some food for herself.

Suddenly she saw her chance. Swooping down right in front of the duck, she seized a crust and flew delightedly with it to the edge of the snow-covered bank. The cat crept up behind her, preparing to pounce. In a flash Peter turned.

"Look out!" he shouted, clapping his hands. Startled, the bird flew back to the tree, while the cat, furious, fluffed out his tail and glared crossly up at her. The duck quacked and flapped her wings but didn't stop eating the chunks of bread still floating on the water.

At this moment Grandfather came striding out of the house, his face red with anger.

"How many times have I told you never to go outside the garden wall alone?" he bellowed at Peter. "What would you do if one day a wolf came out of the forest? Think of that, my boy!" And seizing Peter by the arm, he pulled him back inside the gate, which he shut and locked with a big key he had hanging from his belt.

Grandfather didn't know how soon his fearful warning would come true! Hardly had he and Peter disappeared inside the house than a large, lean wolf came slinking silently out of the trees and across the frozen meadow up to the edge of the pond.

The bird shrilled a warning. The cat in terror leaped up the tree to sit next to the bird. Only the duck was left, and she, silly creature, lost her head completely. Instead of staying in the middle of the pond, she squawked and flapped out of the water and onto the bank. In one quick move the wolf was on her and swallowed the poor duck whole.

Still hungry, the wolf looked about for more. His eye was caught by a movement above his head, and gazing up he saw the cat and the bird huddled together. The wolf stretched up on his hind legs, but the branch was well out of reach. He tried to jump, but still the branch was too high. Finally he started weaving around and around the tree, his narrow yellow eyes fixed on his prey, willing them to fall into his jaws.

Peter had heard the bird's shrill warning and the squawking of the duck. Alarmed by the noise, then by the sudden silence, he ran out of the house and saw at once what had happened. Darting back inside, he returned with a length of strong rope. He jumped onto the garden wall and from there climbed up into the tree where the cat and the bird were cowering.

Peter's plan was daring but simple. He knotted one end of the rope into a lasso. Then he told the bird to swoop down and fly about the wolf's head to distract his attention.

"But be careful," warned Peter. "Keep well clear of those sharp teeth!"

The bird did exactly as Peter instructed, darting and fluttering as near the wolf as she dared. The wolf, enraged, snapped and snarled and twisted and turned, but the bird was too quick for him. Meanwhile, Peter quietly lowered the rope. Then, with one swift jerk, he lassoed the wolf by the neck. The wolf writhed in fury, further ensnaring himself in the rope. His howls of rage brought Grandfather running from the house to stare in amazement at the scene before him.

Just then the sound of a horn rang through the clearing and a couple of hunters appeared from out of the forest. They had been on the trail of the same wolf that now lay roped and helpless at the foot of the tree.

"Don't shoot!" called Peter. "We have caught the wolf. Help us take him to the zoo."

This was Peter's moment of triumph. He led the little procession on its way, a proud smile on his face. Immediately behind him walked the hunters, carrying the wolf on a pole between them. Next came Grandfather, his face as red with pride as before it had been red with anger. Then followed the cat, tail in air, and finally the bird, singing blithely, bringing up the rear. As the little party disappeared up the road and over the hill, the quacking of the duck could be heard growing fainter and fainter in the wolf's belly. . . .